Remembrance of Beauty

By the Same Author:

Love's Dawn

Gaze the Moon

The Ring of Azurmus

Remembrance

of

Beauty

Andrew Chiniche

Reflective
Light
Press

Remembrance of Beauty by Andrew Chiniche

Published by Reflective Light Press
Copyright © 2021 Andrew Chiniche

First Edition: April 2021
Printed in the United States of America

Library of Congress Control Number: 2020924942

Paperback ISBN: 978-1-7326824-3-6
Hardback ISBN: 978-1-7326824-4-3

Edited by Eva Zen
Cover by FrinaArt

Contents

I.   Case File #900509   1

II.   A Midnight Assignation   7

III.   Case File #900509 (2)   15

IV.   The Debut of Alayna Grace   23

V.   Case File #900509 (3)   35

VI.   A Thin Line Between   45

VII. Case File #900509 (4)   53

VIII. A Gentlemen's Discussion   59

IX.   Case File #900509 (5)   65

X.   Harvesting the Fruits   71

XI.   Case File #900509 (6)   77

XII. Remembrance of Beauty   83

Case File #900509 Addendum

I.	Seeing a glimpse	91
II.	My lips paint a picture	92
III.	I smile at the radiance	93
IV.	I see a future path devoid	94
V.	I wish to tear down the barrier	95
VI.	There is a perfection in your lips	96
VII.	Nothing is more intoxicating	97
VIII.	There is a void in my heart	98
IX.	You are the beauty of my life	99
X.	I want to bite your neck	100
XI.	Your beauty burns	101
XII.	All barriers have eroded	102
XIII.	You are my waking dream	103
XIV.	Magick is captured	104

XV.	The time has arrived	105
XVI.	As a beacon burns	106
XVII.	Our intermingled sweat	107
XVIII.	With a deep breath	108
XIX.	Tie a bind across my eyes	109
XX.	Communicate your secrets	110
XXI.	You are my fierce sexy angel	111
XXII.	I wake up with the dream	112
XXIII.	After falling to my knees	113
XXIV.	Your secret beauty	114
XXV.	The sun of your soul rises	115
XXVI.	Your beauty enchants	116
XXVII.	Like a comet burning	117
XXVIII.	Cages of flesh	118

XXIX.	You are the gateway	119
XXX.	Beauty overwhelms	120
XXXI.	Residual memories	121
XXXII.	There is perfection	122
XXXIII.	My heart sings out	123
XXXIV.	With a glance at the sun	124
XXXV.	To write about you	125
XXXVI.	Oh God	126
XXXVII.	With a thought	127
XXXVIII.	As the river of time widens	128
XXXIX.	The idea of you	129
XL.	I wonder	130

Restoration

1. the act of restoring or state of being restored, as to a former or original condition.

2. the replacement or giving back of something lost, stolen.

3. something restored, replaced, or reconstructed.

Collins English Dictionary – Complete and Unabridged
© HarperCollins Publishers 1991, 1994, 1998, 2000, 2003

I.

Case File #900509

...I remember Beauty.

Was she punished for that?
What a strange thing to punish someone for...

All men desire to possess
and wallow in beauty.

If beauty is within one's grasp,
but then escapes,
it must be destroyed.

What great crime did she commit?
Did she spurn beauty?
Was she beautiful?

The mists of the past
float in my mind,
and I have no clear picture.

She is a fixture,
maybe an obsession,
in my brain.

I want to see her face again.
(Double CLICK! as a briefcase opens)
What do you have?

Stop.
Please stop.
I do not want to see.
PUT THE PICTURE AWAY!

What are you trying to do?
That's not her.

Her real essence is not there.
Pictures are just particles
arranged on shiny paper.

The only way to really see
the true her is to remember.

To free myself,
I need her real essence
as she was.

What was that?
Please tell me what you said.
Did I feel guilty?

I will tell you about guilt.
Guilt grows from shame, disgust, and regret.
I have not experienced these sensations.

Why are you so shocked?
My feelings for her do not involve guilt.
Do not project your reasons for being onto me.

I obsess over her
so I may take back
what she stole from me.

I know.
I killed her.
What of it?

I took her life, but she took
so much more from me.
That was the point of what I did.

Her death was a mistake.
She should have lived;
I need her to live.

That's why I must pull her image
and being, from my brain.

I need her back in my life.
I just wanted to take back
what she stole from me.

It was not a tangible object.
She did not even know
she had taken anything.

Do not judge me.
I was completely justified in my actions.

Do you want my explanations?
Read my file.
I have already told them to you once.

Oh...
I see.

This is how you help.

I must retread through the past
to forge a path to a new
and brighter future?

Okay...
I will.

II.

A Midnight Assignation

(Chicago, 1923)

Lying in bed after midnight,
the idea of sleep eludes me
as the humid city air clings to my skin.

A vicious pounding
on our brownstone entrance
rattles the house.

Muffled voices of veiled rage
speak to my father in tones of menace.

After agreeing to accompany them,
the known associates allow
a moment before leaving.

My father's heavy steps tread upstairs
and echo into my room.

The frantic tears of mother
reach my ears
as my doorknob jangles.

With a rush of fabric,
I pull the covers over my head,
leaving one eye free.

My bedroom door creaks open,
and I glimpse as he looks at me
before heading back down.

Springing to my window,
I watch as they saunter
towards the repair shop,
my father sandwiched between them.

Pulling on my pants
and snapping my suspenders into place,
I slip into a jacket and slink
out the window onto the fire escape.
I glide to the pavement without a sound.

Staying in the murkiness of shadows,
I creep behind bus benches
and hide in alcoves.

After they enter though a side door,
I scale the wall and climb to a perch.
Looking through a dormer window,
I see the expanse of the garage floor.

The goons sit my father
in a chair under a naked bulb.

It swings after the string is pulled.
Hulks of cars skirt on the edge
of the projected shadows.

A third gentlemen hovers
on the fringe with a hint of his body
in dad's line of sight.

Mumbled questions vibrate
to my hearing through the glass.

My father emphatically shakes his head
in the signal of "no"
as he tries to wave them off.

An open ham hock fist smacks across his face
splattering blood in a flowing arc.
Somehow, he absorbs the force
and remains seated on the chair.

Repeated questions hurl through the air
and the pantomime continues.

Smack!
An eye swells purple.

Slap!
Nose brakes.

Smash!
Lips balloon.

The leader cradles my father's mangled face,
and, like a lover, whisperers close.

Sitting limply,
dad moves his head back and forth
again signaling a negative response.

The goons watch as rage explodes
through their boss's body.

He reaches to the small of his back,
whips a revolver from his waste-band,
and shoves it into my father's mouth.

The world becomes a slow blur
as tears stream down my face.

A final volley of words flies
through the aggressor's lips
as a cloud of red mist explodes.

Brain matter splatters to the floor.

A cold clarity freezes over my body
as the gunman howls at the hanging bulb
and is caught in a beam of raw light.

All of us have seen him around.
He is the neighborhood bootlegger.
Sometimes, he'll flip us a half-dollar
as we play stick ball in the street.

The visage of "Bear" Sullivan
burns into my memory.
The seed of revenge embeds
into the fertile soil of my soul.

I sit in my crow's nest sinking in grief
until the soft glow of the coming sun
pierces the edge of the horizon.

I go home in a daze.
After entering the kitchen,
I see my mother
at the breakfast table.

She sits in a smog of cigarette smoke
with a hill of ash between us.

As I walk past and towards the stairs,
I tell her I am not going to school today.

She nods languidly in agreement without looking.

III.

Case File #900509
Cont'd

What is the purpose of living?
Are we here to leave our mark?
Do bums have the right idea?

Maybe they do.

I discovered my purpose.
You could call it my "special purpose",
but then I'm not a jerk.

I am to elevate mankind
by rescuing the forgotten things.

A man of any worth must create himself
and mold the world into his own image.

I do not care about helping others.
Helping others is an unintended
side effect of my actions.

Since bums are the best
people to do nothing with,
I walk down to Bienville
and find a bench to lounge on.

It just takes a couple of hours,
and everything is better in your life.

The entire downtown,
from the bums to the buildings,
is a study in atrophy.

Look at the architecture surrounding the Square.

Imagine the buildings in their heyday:
Fresh, new, and important.
Now: empty and mossy.

What happened?

The bums and buildings lost their hope.
That's what happened,
but there's still a chance.

Each has forgotten their hidden potential.
All it takes is just a little kick
or a slight push
and
POOF!
There it is.

I want to be the one
to save the bums
and the buildings.

Everything deserves to reach
its true, full potential.

And the City agrees with me!

Well... mostly.

The new mayor and the city council
want to save the buildings to restore downtown
back to its previous glory through the newly formed
"String of Pearls" initiative.

This initiative began as a way
to help me save downtown.

Unfortunately, the bums,
being more barnacles than pearls,
do not fit into *their* vision for the City
and are to be removed instead of saved.

I will follow the city council's lead
and give up on the bums too.

No great loss, really—
And besides...
...they just smell bad.

Anyway, buildings are easier to save than people.

I have the perfect place to start:
the abandoned Sullivan mansion.

It's an old Victorian
with a gabled roof
and a wrap-around porch
abandoned for more
than a month of years.

If you look closely,
the for-sale sign is buried up to its bar
in crab grass and dandelions.

The aura of scandal and loss is tactile.

Before my purchase,
I leap into all the history
and rumors that I can find.

This place is great!

The realtor did a double take
when I told him I wanted to purchase
the old derelict house.

It's normal that places
with unsavory histories never sell,
but I bought the place,
and there is no turning back.

My past intertwines
with the Sullivan House,
and she became the nexus point.

What?

No.

This is *not* a ghost story.
You know that already.
This is all in my file.

Just let me tell this the way I want to.
Remember.
This is "helping" me.

IV.

The Debut of Alayna Grace
(Mobile, 1939)

As I sit for my portrait,
time travels tediously.
I feel like a statue.

The spring sun courses
through the majestic old oaks
with their branches tracing
shadows over the Square.

The rumble of traffic
zips past on Dauphin Street.
The exhaust fumes tickle my nose.

Behind me, at an intersection of walkways,
a four-tier verdigris fountain
towers towards the sky.

As I hear the musical song of water,
I imagine the sparkling arch fly in the air
and splash on the surface of the pool.

The weight of an open parasol
rests on my shoulder,
it's filigree edging similar
to the ruffles of my ivory dress.

I absorb the spirit of downtown:
the phantoms of Mardi Gras,
the echoes of the Civil War,
the residue of six flags.

"Miss Alayna Grace, please
bring your chin down a bit."

I do as the artist commands.

"Perfect."

Papa commissioned this painting
in celebration of my coming birthday.

It's an extravagant expense,
but he overcompensates
for the death of my mother.

It's been two years
since consumption took her.
A hollow sadness sometimes engulfs me.

I've been hidden away
in Bishop Toolen's school for girls.

Although the nuns can be scary,
I've enjoyed my tenure there.

The time has arrived
to introduce myself to the world.
The coming celebration will
welcome me to adult society.
It's a ball of fancy dress and dancing.

Since I've always been fascinated
by the pair of Sphinx that guard the entrance,
I wanted my grand event held
at the Scottish Rite Temple
on Saint Francis Street.

Just as the Egyptian pharaohs entombed
their afterlife in imposing pyramids,
I wanted a suitable place to bury my childhood.

———

With the last wisps
of the setting sun
streaking across the sky,
the gathering starts at seven.

As the hostess and honored guest,
I scurry about meeting and greeting.
Mindless conversation spouts in spurts.

Before the dancing begins,
father wants to reveal
the artistic endeavor he financed.

With colorful crepe paper
streaming from the ceiling,
we stand on stage for the reveal.

I scan the audience
and see many of my school friends
among members of the glitterati.
Everyone gazes in anticipation.

I am slightly embarrassed
by his meandering speech.
The words are a blur,
but he expresses his deeply held sentiment.

Between my father and I,
the portrait lies hidden
under a heavy drape.

He uses a rope pulley system to lift the sheet.
After a sharp tug of a dangling appendage,
the covering levitates into the air.

I see myself stare at me.
It is surreal in a detached sort of way.
Like Dorian, I will be forever young.

The bombardment of applause
causes my cheeks to burnish crimson.

With a flourish of his hand,
father motions for the band
to strike up a tune.

He leads me to the center of the room
in a waltz-type fox trot.

After a moment of allowing us space,
the crowd soon follows
and the floor is bustling.

As I am twirled and whirled around,
a pair of captivating eyes
catch my attention.

With each rotation,
I am pulled deeper into their allure.
I almost drown in the stormy sea
brewing around his pupils.

The evening wears on,
and I work at the task of
emptying my dance card.

The earlier excitement of scheduling my partners
has vacated with my new discovery.
I know he hovers on my periphery.

At a lull in the music,
flush from my excursions,
I am in need of a refreshment.

As one of my girlfriends
distracts me with her yammering,
I reach for a glass of punch.

Instead of the cool chill of a sweaty glass,
I feel the warmth of a calloused hand
gently enveloping my fingers.

His lips caress my knuckles
and he whispers,
"Hello. My name is Guy.
Will you come with me?"

I nod yes.

The buzz of the revelers falls away
as a bubble of silence separates
us from them.

We move into the inner Temple
with the weight of the darkened
corridors pressing upon us.

After many maze-like twists and turns,
we enter a room two floors higher than the party.
The moon streams through an uncovered window.

With our bodies pressed together,
his face is a mask of shadows.
A tense strength courses through his limbs.

"Please forgive me if I speak out of line,
but I am transfixed by your beauty.

I...
I do not want to seem forward...
I love you.

As the fair princess gives her champion
a token of her esteem,
I hope you will give me a kiss.

Only then will I know I'm not a fool.
Only then will I have the courage
to see you again upon the morrow."

I tilt back my head and close my eyes.
His full lips embrace mine
in a sensual chasteness.

My heartbeat increases
as the moment stretches into eternity.

We disengage and I take a step back.
The music drifts in a soft echo.

"Dance with me."

He bows gracefully
and takes me by the hand.

"My pleasure."

With the phantom beat as our guide
and the moon as our spotlight,
we keep time and grow closer.

I could have danced all night…

V.

Case File #900509
Cont'd

Close your eyes.
You need to see to understand.

Come on.

Just.
      Trust.
            Me.

I don't wanna hurt you.

Humor me.
Please.

Remember:
You must help me to help *me*.

Now.

Lightly close your eyes
and empty your mind.

You are standing on
North Joachim Street,
facing the Sullivan house.

Look at the whole house and absorb it.

The crumbling concrete walkway
reverts into separate rocks.

Debris scatters around the yard:
cans, glass, and old newspapers
with sprigs of crabgrass and dandelions
popping up sporadically.

The porch sags with the paint flaking off,
the windows are jagged eyes,
and the roof is a ruin of pockmarked tiles.

The shutters are missing or hanging askew.
Through the broken and cracked windows,
leaves and trash blew in.

Since it was abandoned,
the house has sheltered
many bums and homeless people.

These outcasts and rejects treated the house crudely:
Trash, crap, and dirt were its reward
for helping these poor people out.

I intend to restore the abode
to its prime by going to the past.

The decaying house is a synthesis
between nature's chaos
and man's ordered beauty.

The house has become a new form—
One that man despises.

I have been chosen to cultivate this new form.
Let's call it "fusion beauty."

I want the house to regain its old vitality,
but without removing the knowledge
it has gained through years of existence.

Most people would go
into an old house
and gut everything.

I cannot do that.

The house earned its scars and its personality;
I will not change it completely.

I rent a dumpster,
and park it in the back yard.

My mission is to empty the house
of this accumulated foreign matter.

The process begins in the great room,
the heart of the house.
Think of it as a bypass surgery.

The 12-foot-high ceiling is
composed of hand-carved tiles
placed in an interconnected pattern.

Beneath the dust,
the wall panels gleam
with a dark-burled wood.

Lighter shadows of dirt and grime
show, where at one time, pictures hung.

Only one painting remains.
Over the fireplace, it is covered
in a thick sheen of physical time.

With the soft sweeping of a bristled brush,
I use meticulous stokes to reveal the waiting treasure.

A beautiful damsel
poses under a majestic southern oak
with moss draping its branches.

A parasol rests over her shoulder
with a fountain in the background.
All painted in an impressionistic style.

The fountain is the one from the Square.
Take her out, put in a couple of bums,
and that's the Bienville I'm used to.

I feel the girl calling me;
She's the reason I purchased this house.

The room was created to showcase her.

When standing at its very center,
the view of the portrait is perfect.

As the setting sun burns through the great window,
the strands of her hair float and move about.

I feel the warm wafting breeze of summer
flow from the day the paint captured her.

Her soft features,
delicate and inviting,
live as the day's light dies.

I watch until the sun
transitions through dusk
and away into night.

I feel trapped in a daze
as my soul drifts through lost decades.

.
.
.

POP!
            POP!

I roll to the floor
as two bullets fly by my head,
ringing out from the mantel.

The crumpling thump of a body
sounds behind me.

With everything wavy and hazy,
I gaze up from the floor.
A gaping wound bleeds from her chest.

.

.

.

The morning sun streams
and I wake up.

Stiff and worn from a night on the floor,
I look around the room.

Everything is dirty and grimy
except the girl with the parasol.
She is beautiful and not wounded.

Nothing has changed except my experience.

What happened last night?
The dust must have messed up my head.
It's time for a good soak at my apartment's hot tub.

VI.

A Thin Line Between
(Mobile, 1939)

Since my quest for revenge
absorbs my waking moments,
I cannot help her.

Mother never recovered
from the murder of my father.
She faded as her inner fire cooled.

Shortly after Bear moved his family,
I leave her in the care of my aunt,
and follow him to the port city.

Through patience and fortitude,
my path opens before me.
I support myself with odd jobs
and always being available.

Using sharpened scissors,
I trim the announcement
from the Register's society page.

ALEXANDER "BEAR" SULLIVAN
CELEBRATES HIS DAUGHTER,
ALAYNA GRACE.

HAPPY BIRTHDAY GALA!

GUEST INVITATIONS FORTHCOMING.
GALLERY TICKETS AVAILABLE.

The invited guests and his daughter
will witness my judgement.
I resolve for him to die
in the midst of celebration.

After years of honing my hatred,
the time of retribution arrives.

———

With the moon reflecting
on the polished midnight of my shoes,
I wear formal tails, a black tie,
and a starched white shirt.
A red carnation adorns my lapel.

Without a care in the world,
I walk through the front entrance.
The muffled music echoes into the street.

Shaking hands with people I pretend to know,
my forward momentum carries me
into the ballroom.

As the crowd quiets to a murmur,
the object of my obsession
joyfully takes the stage.

Tunnel vision takes hold of me
and I see Bear in a cold clarity.

I finger the handle of my pistol
to reassure myself.

The sound of his words floats to my ears,
but I do not discern their meaning.
My brain rehearses my intention.

I pull the gun from its hidden holster
and squeeze the trigger.

A cloud of black power propels the bullet
through the muzzle flash.

A look of confusion furrows Bear's brow
as the brilliant ball buries itself
under his eye socket.

A perfect circle,
singed around the edges,
leaks a crimson tear
from its dark abyss.

An explosion of red gore spatters
a Rorschach pattern upon the wall.
His inert body collapses in a heap.

I snap from my reverie
as Bear reaches above him
and pulls a rope.

With a sheet's swoosh and the release of balloons,
my attention becomes distracted.
An angel, captured in oils, is revealed.

The world freezes before me
as the twin of the painting,
real flesh and blood,
enters my ever-expanding focus.

As my breath quickens,
my accelerated heartbeat
turns my cheeks crimson.

A barrage of arrows
lets loose from Cupid's bow
and unleashes my hidden ardor.

My hand drifts away from my gun,
its purpose and existence forgotten.

She curtseys to the crowd in thanks,
Bear takes her by the hand,
and they begin to dance.
We form a circle around them.

She radiates happiness and smiles.
Her life source pulls me like gravity;
I am a planet to her sun.

In one of her twirling spins,
she glances towards me.

Our eyes lock with allure.
Eternity lives in a gaze of amber gold.

The circle of people breaks up
and the audience transforms into participants.

I move into the shadows
amongst the wall flowers,
but I never lose sight of her.

As the belle of the ball,
she's busy entertaining
and being the center of attention.

My opportunity arises
when, in a brief break,
she walks over to the punch table
trailing a girlfriend behind her.

Absorbed in conversation,
her blind hand snakes along,
searching for a cup of liquid.

After capturing her fingers in a loose grasp,
I bring her knuckles to my lips and whisper:
"Hello. My name is Guy.
Will you come with me?"

———

With the buzz of Alayna
coursing through my veins,
I wake up hungover on emotion.

The swirling around my brain
empowers me to want her more.
I cannot wait to see her this afternoon!

VII.

Case File #900509
Cont'd

After finally removing the trash and debris,
I make a discovery:

Lofty ideas of salvation
only fulfill half our needs.

To be whole, we must not only give in to,
but wallow in, our basest desires.

Wallowing acts as a cleansing agent
and removes the drivel our brains
get mired in as we trudge through life.

A year elapses,
and I cannot bring myself
to disturb the beautiful entropy
that envelopes the property.

Maybe, if I return to the starting point,
I will have a better feel of how to proceed.

Back at Bienville, I use my balled up
jacket as a pillow and lounge on a bench.

Since being around bums makes me invisible,
she does not see me as I spy her
mysterious aura trail through the park.

Like a Romantic age heroine,
she flows by tall and slender
with alabaster skin and ruby lips.

Every day I watch for her,
and she does not disappoint.

Gazing from afar is safer than action,
but nothing is gained without risk.

I will not bore you
with my "boy meets girl" story.

You just need to know that
our relationship began
as a mutual understanding.

At least, I understood what I was doing.
She either wanted to explore life, to punish her father,
or a maybe a twisted combination of both.

When you boil away the fat
from our relationship,
here is the key:

She wanted to fuck around with the house
and I wanted to fuck her.

I know it's a little bit vulgar,
but I am trying to be honest.

VIII.

A Gentlemen's Discussion

(Mobile, 1940)

A nervous tremor vibrates
through my person
as Bear's glacier gaze pierces.

He stands by the fireplace
beneath Alayna's portrait,
warming a brandy in his hand.

I sit across from him
on the bay window bench.

"Alayna and I want to marry,
but before asking your permission,
I need to tell you something.

I know what you did in Chicago.

I watched from a dormer window
as you beat and then murdered my father.

My original driving force
was to exact revenge,
but love destroyed my hate.

Will you allow me to protect
and care for your daughter,

knowing that I was once your enemy?"

The blood drains from Bear's face,
and I cannot tell if it's from my revealed secret
or my intentions towards his girl.

He despondently lifts the brandy to his lips.

After an excruciating slow sip,
he lets the snifter drop
and reaches under his vest.

During my monologue,
stress stored in my guts
like tension in a clock spring.

With the decent of the glass,
I unleash my stored energy
and rush towards him.

After freeing the gun from his belt's entanglement,
he causes a shot to ring out:

BANG!

The bullet splinters the floor at my feet.

Using my whole body,
and my accumulated momentum,
I slam into Bear, pushing his gun into the mantle.

He manages to squeeze off two rounds.

    POP!

        POP!

They wiz along the length of room
with a burning buzz.

Behind me and to the left,
I hear a sharp intake of breath
and a murmur of

    "Why?"

followed by a bodily thump.

IX.

Case File #900509

Cont'd

We enter the threshold
with our hands almost touching.
The tentacles of our auras intertwine.

Does she know what's coming?
Does she feel complete around me?
I feel it and I'm willing to share.

As the dying sunlight pushes
its way through the windows,
I lead her into the great room.

With one hand at the small of her back,
we engage in a slow ritualistic dance.

The pulse of the house serves
as our internal song's rhythm.

The curve of her neck flows
as her ivory summer dress
exposes her muscular back.

In a symphony of sensual movements,
her legs flirt with exposure
as the slit of her dress
threatens to open wider.

Two red roses embroidered high over her breast
seem to beat as the blood rushes through my veins.

She holds a parasol like a cane.
It tap, tap, taps on the wooden floor
as we progress around the room.

The past bends around us
like a crease folded in paper.

I feel the rage of Bear boil
as I slap open my switchblade.

Holding her hand
to keep her in place.
I thrust manically.
Flesh parts like canvas.

A wordless bellow escapes my lips,
punctuating the piercing of my shiny steel.

She is strangely silent
as her frame breaks down
and crumples to the floor.

———

Her death came quicker than expected.
The entire ordeal was meant to be a sort of joke,
maybe a lesson or a simple warning.

I can't remember any longer.

Time, along with reflection,
should work to make past actions
and thoughts clearer,
but the reasons behind what I did
are rippled and grey.

I cannot focus.

If they let me out of here,
I'm sure the correct answer
will make itself known.

It must.
     Right?

The unknown and the once known scratch
and claw its way to my mind's surface
to make its way into being.

Everything has a desire to be true and real,
even old forgotten justifications.

Do you think she suffered?

I want her to understand what she did.

This was not a childish fancy,
but a balancing of the scales.

X.

Harvesting the Fruits

(Mobile, 1940)

I feel Bear's gaze follow mine
as we both look towards the hollow thud.
His daughter crumples on the floor.

I release Bear, hurry over,
and scoop Alayna into my arms.

Blood bubbles from her month
as she tries to speak.

Her amber fire dims,
smolders a last brightness,
and finally fades away.

Cold black emptiness
stares into my eyes.

[As Bear watches in a dumbfounded stupor,
he still clutches his pistol.

His actions have brought about
the worst possible outcome.

Seven years ago, he left bootlegging
and its business behind
and traveled to a new place

to forge a safe, secure future.

Now:
His wife, taken from him by illness.
His lovely daughter, dead by his own hand.
She was his heart.
She was his soul.
She was all that mattered.

Nothing exists anymore except his guilt.]

Tears drown my eyes
as her body cools in my arms.
Noiseless sobs heave from my chest.

[As he fights his gag reflex,
the steel barrel tastes of spent gunpowder.

With a glance at the separated lovers,
he tests the trigger's tension,
takes a deep breath,
and commits to oblivion.

POW!

The red and gray gore splatters the wall.
Its grotesque ugliness stands out in contrast

74

to the beauty of Alayna's portrait,
where she will be eternally young.]

With the gun's final explosion,
I fall back and nearly drop my beloved.
Bear's body slides down the wall
and slumps to the floor.

A fresh clarity comes to me:
I cannot explain tonight's happenings
without jeopardizing myself.

I disentangle from Alayna's body
and lay her on the floor in a gentle repose.

I notice a lace handkerchief
tucked in her waistband.

After taking it in hand,
I see a script monogram
embroidered in the center.

I dip a corner in her blood,
and stuff it in my pocket
to always have a part of her.

I bend over her body
and caress her lips with mine.

They are so supple.
She seems to live.

As I exit the Sullivan house,
the back-screen door bangs like thunder.

XI.

Case File #900509

Final Assessment

"You've been allowed
this fantasy long enough.
It's time to face reality.

The owners of the Sullivan House
had run out of money during renovations
and left it semi-abandoned.

You lived among the homeless
and would use it as a shelter.

As you loitered there,
you became obsessed
with the painting of Miss Alayna.

She is the girl you saw in the park
and you imagined the entire relationship.

On the night of the supposed incident,
the police found you huddled in Bienville Square,
clutching a sheaf of poems,
and mumbling about your guilt.

You left a trail of sheets
torn from the bundle
leading back to the house.

Instead of finding a perforated corpse,
a shredded painting with a crumpled frame
lay in a heap on the floor.

A few more loose pages
were discovered nearby.

It has not been determined where the poems
came from, but you did not write them.

You are not a murderer
because there wasn't a dead girl.

We have allowed you to tell your story
in the hope your delusion would fade
and the true truth would occur to you.

Since that has not happened,
it has been recommended
that we change your course of treatment.

Unless you can convince me
to change their minds,
electroshock therapy will be
administered once daily for a week.

It is up to you.
Do you have anything to tell me?"

...I remember Beauty.

XII.

Remembrance of Beauty

(Mobile, 1980)

Alayna never left my memory.
Her countenance haunts my dreams
and influences my being.

As my path journeys towards my end,
I need to return to where she left her life,
and bask in the remembrance of her.

With debris scattered over the grounds,
there is no one around.
A for-sale sign floats above long crab grass.

I enter through the way I left,
and notice signs of recent work:
a dumpster in the back,
track marks through dust,
tools scattered about.

I kneel where she last laid
and trace the maroon stain
with my fingertips.
I can almost feel her skin's silkiness.

Struggling to stand,
weak from sorrow and old age,
I make my way to her portrait.

There is no trace of residue to indicate
the two score years between us.

I sometimes think her death was my fault.
If I'd only asked for her hand
and not brought up the past connection.

I cannot dwell on that.
Destiny led me to that point
and fate pushed the outcome.

I see the sun of summer
glow around her
as she stands in Bienville.

She is the beauty that fills my life.
Her spark lives and radiates
on the exhale of my breath.

As I caress the texture of the paint,
my hand trembles from either from palsy
or suppressed excitement.
I'm not sure which.

I withdraw a thin bundle from my satchel
and thread it under the corner of the frame.

An emotional outpouring captured in ink.
My love for her is everlasting.

As I turn to leave,
I can feel the warmth of Alayna's gaze
and the happiness of her smile
rain from her portrait.

Having learned from Orpheus,
I do not turn for a final look
and exit by the front door
like an honored guest.

Case File #900509

Addendum

After analysis, the handwriting is consistent on all the poems using a blue-black fountain pen ink. The iron oxide in the ink shows various degrees of aging. From this evidence, we believe the same person wrote these poems over several years.

I.

Seeing a glimpse of your face
imparts life's hidden beauty.

You are the mystery
I want to be a part of.

II.

My lips paint a picture
across the valleys of your body.

Wonderment lies in every curve.

Let us celebrate the new dawn
by wallowing in the magick of flesh.

III.

I smile at the radiance
of your beauty.

You are a wispy dream
living in my waking thoughts.

I miss the whisper of your voice
and your feather touch.

I'd love to spend time with you again.

IV.

I see a future path devoid of companionship,
but I will always feel your presence.

You lurk around my edges
and in my heart.

Please see yourself the way I do:
You are beauty,
you are love,
you are enough.

Do you feel our connection
as I hold you tight?

V.

I wish to tear down the barrier
and let someone in,
but I cannot.

I am always a fingerbreadth away
from unlatching the door.

VI.

There is a perfection on your lips
that cannot be matched.

My happiness lives on the whisper
of your breath.

Say my name
and let me sigh your praises.

Time spent not kissing you is time wasted.

VII.

Nothing is more intoxicating
than a Muse's inspiration.

I merge my soul
with each word and phrasing
to pen epics in your honor.

VIII.

There is a void in my heart
that pulls towards
the electricity of your essence.

To kiss the fullness of your lips
and breathe of your air…
That is my wish.

I need to be near you.
I need to worship you.
I need to love you.

Will you share of my communion?

IX.

You are the beauty of my life.

Although there are miles between us,
your essence surrounds me
and I feel at peace.

X.

I want to bite your neck.

Just barely.

Just enough to feel your pulse beat.
The roughness of your skin drives me wild.

Your taste is intoxicating.

As you turn your face towards mine,
I attack your lips.

I love kissing you
and could do so forever.
A slight moment of eternal heaven.

XI.

Your beauty burns sweetly in my soul.
I am forever marked.
Your kiss is the only balm that will soothe me.

XII.

All barriers have eroded.

Leave your body
and join my essence
on the edge of time.

Use me as your pleasure dome.

XIII.

You are my waking dream!

The force of your beauty overwhelms me.
To taste your kiss again…

XIV.

Magick is captured in your countenance.
I love to gaze at your picture and dream.

I dream of holding you.
I dream of your kiss.
I dream of passion.

I want to dive into the fantasy of you
and never emerge.

Take my hand
and help me to drown in pleasure.
Heaven lives with in you.

XV.

The time has arrived
to rend the fabric of the universe
and destroy the distance between us.

I want to walk out my door
and into your arms.

Our reunion will create balance.
The shape of you fits
into the puzzle of my heart.

XVI.

As a beacon burns in the night,
you light the path to my future.

I love the excitement of you:
holding you tight,
kissing your lips,
being near your touch.

Let me soak in your aura
and complete the circuit of my soul.

XVII.

Our intermingled sweat
glistens as it cools,
causing me to shiver.

You lay in the crook of my arm
with your head on my chest
and warm me with your body.

I play with your hair
and absorb your scent.

Time has stopped
and we are the world.

This is the fleeting forever,
our moment of eternity.

XVIII.

With a deep breath,
I intake the idea of you;
I let it fill me.

Beauty lives in your essence
and I need it.

I need it to enhance my being.
I need it to fulfill my dreams.
I need it because I need *you*.

XIX.

Tie a bind across my eyes
and make me taste your perfection.

I trace your country of curves
with your sighs to guide me.

As a bat with sonar,
I search for your pleasure points.

My tongue finally settles into your valley
to discover the joy of you.

XX.

Communicate your secrets with your lips,
and engulf me in the fire of your passion.

I want to be absorbed by you.

Feed me your breath
and give me life.

You are me
and I am you.
We are eternal.

XXI.

You are my fierce sexy angel.
Your power keeps me enchanted.

I always look for your radiance
in my pursuit of beauty.

XXII.

I wake up with the dream
of your kiss on my lips.

I trace with my tongue
to recapture the memory.
I need to indulge in you!

XXIII.

After falling to my knees,
I call out to the exalted one
and send a vibration into the air.

The universe is made of balance,
and I search for my counterpart.

I gaze at you
and catch a glimpse of eternity.

Do you accept my anima?

XXIV.

Your secret beauty is hidden
in the recess of your soul.

Share it with me.

Reach out and let me feel of your spirit.
I need the essence of you.

XXV.

The sun of your soul rises,
and I feel how exquisite you are.

Burn me with your fire.

I must caress the spark of life;
The source lies within you.

XXVI.

Your beauty enchants
and heightens my awareness.

I forget about the world
as you surround me
in your magickal bubble.

Take me by the hand
and let me embrace the comfort of you.

XXVII.

Like a comet burning through space,
the golden light of your eyes appears before me.

I feel their brilliance look through my façade
and gaze into my essence.

The force of your beauty guides my life.

XXVIII.

Let us give up our cages of flesh
and float beyond the corporal world,
a place of confusion and dissolution.

In our higher selves, we can be free,
and meld in love's light,
a substance of purity and strength.

As I wait for the time of emancipation,
I dream of you,
the embodiment of light.

Through the beating of your heart,
love flows in the world,
and I need you.

XXIX.

You are the gateway
to infinite bliss.

Fuse your passion's energy with mine
and help me transcend the mundane.

In a cloud of ecstatic joy,
I breathe of your breath
and experience your radiant beauty.

Eternity lives in your kiss.

XXX.

Beauty overwhelms
and lifts me.

My soul stirs from its slumber
as my third eye envisions you.

I capture the inspiration bestowed upon me
and rise to unknown heights.

You embody transcendent womanhood.

XXXI.

I am free in residual memories.

You dance in the waves of ecstasy
that caress the shores of my heart.

As your beauty elevates me to the stratosphere,
my worship sees the divine in you.

XXXII.

There is perfection in your form,
and I love you.

I love your curves.
I love your strength.
I love your beauty.

Waves of emotions wash over me
and bring me to my knees.

Like a strike of lightening
with ozone burning the air,
your image brands my retina.

I see reflections of you
wherever my gaze hovers.

XXXIII.

My heart sings out
and forms the shape of your name.

I feel you next to me
as your spirit exhales.

Breathe deep
and forever be.

Your importance is infinite.

XXXIV.

With a glance at the sun,
I see a flash of you
and celebrate beauty.

XXXV.

To write about you
is to imagine ecstasy.

I want to caress your body
and swim in your mind,
but heaven lives in your lips.

I hope to kiss you forever…
This is my happiness.

XXXVI.

Oh, God!
I want to kiss you again.

Long.
Slow.
Sensual.

XXXVII.

With a thought and a prayer,
I install you in my pantheon.
You are love, light, and passion.

My Aphrodite.

I long to take you as my communion
and partake of your pulsating desire.

XXXVIII.

As the river of time widens
the valley between us,
my thoughts drift back.

An indistinct halo hovers
fusing real and imaginary
into an amalgamation.

A whisper of your name,
and my heart races.

A glimpse of your image,
and I must reach out.

A part of your passion
embeds in my soul.
My love for you radiates.

A word from your lips,
and the answer is yes.

XXXIX.

The idea of you
is always present in my mind.

Your beauty and grace wash
over the shore of my being.

Your prominence is supreme,
and I would be less without you.

I love you like no one else.

XL.

I wonder what it would be like
to kiss you goodnight,
knowing that you are an arm's reach away.

Then, when I wake,
I can hold you,
and feel the warmth of your body
meld with mine
as your soul calms me.

About the Author

Andrew John Chiniche is a self-published author and poet with a vision to add magick to his readers' lives through the power of poetic storytelling. On his lifelong quest of higher truth, he also strives to embolden deep-rooted emotions, inspire deep thought, and invite others to ponder the mysteries of this expansive universe. In addition to authoring four poetry collections (*Love's Dawn*, *Gaze the Moon*, *The Ring of Azurmus*, and *Remembrance of Beauty*), he holds a Bachelor's degree in English Literature from Mississippi State University. When he isn't writing, Andrew enjoys getting lost in the unique worlds of movies and books.